Lulu the Lost Lamb

Dedicated to my Family,
Past, Present and Future.

It was afternoon
and all of the young lambs
were snuggled up
ready to take a nap.

Lulu's Mum Sheba
went to get a drink
from the pond.

A herd of horses moved swiftly in to the valley which frightened the birds and woke Lulu.

Sheba began to look for Lulu.
She walked over a hill and found
a rabbit, who she asked
"Have you seen my Lulu?"

"Not today",
replied the rabbit.

"Kimba, have you seen Lulu?" asked Sheba.

"No, I've been sleeping", replied the koala.

"Hello Cookie, have you seen Lulu? I've been searching for her everywhere."

"No Sheba, but I can organise a search party fly over for you", answered the cockatoo.

"Yes please Cookie!" said Sheba. "A storm is coming!"

The rain began to fall.
Lightning struck!
The thunder rolled through the hills!

"Oh where,
oh where
can my Lulu be?"
asked Sheba out loud.

Mrs. Owl heard Sheba
in her distress.

Sheba heard a voice
that came from
a nearby tree.

"The little ones will hide
where they can.
She would be small enough
to fit in a hollow log.
Have you tried looking in
Wally Wombat's home?"

"No, I haven't.
Oh thank you Mrs. Owl,
I will run there now to look.
I do hope you are right."

"Sheba! We found Lulu!" squawked Cookie excitedly.

"Oh thank you Cookie. Let's go!"

"Follow me! This way!"

"The storm has almost gone." said Cookie.

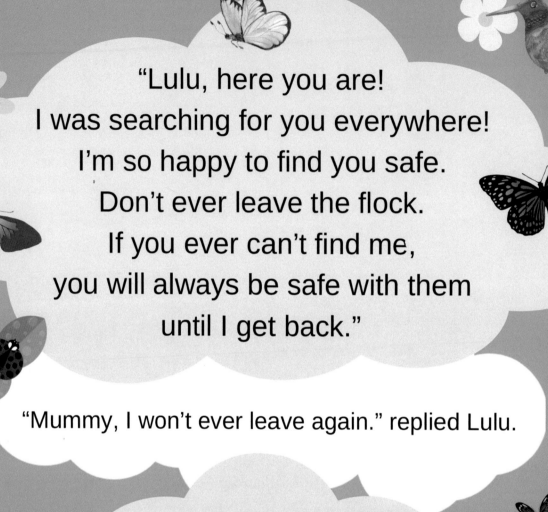

"Lulu, here you are!
I was searching for you everywhere!
I'm so happy to find you safe.
Don't ever leave the flock.
If you ever can't find me,
you will always be safe with them
until I get back."

"Mummy, I won't ever leave again." replied Lulu.

"Thank you Cookie,
your whole flock, Eddie and
wise Mrs. Owl."
said Sheba gratefully.

The Happy Ending

Made in the USA
Las Vegas, NV
14 June 2023

73356541R00019